THE MAILBOX TRICK

D0062541

**Other Apple Paperbacks
by Scott Corbett:**

The Hangman's Ghost Trick
The Hairy Horror Trick
The Disappearing Dog Trick

THE MAILBOX TRICK

Scott Corbett

Illustrated by Paul Galdone

AN
APPLE
PAPERBACK

SCHOLASTIC INC.
New York Toronto London Auckland Sydney

Scholastic Books are available at special discounts for quantity pur-
chases for use as premiums, promotional items, retail sales through
specialty market outlets, etc. For details contact: Special Sales Manager,
Scholastic Inc., 730 Broadway, New York, NY 10003.

No part of this publication may be reproduced in whole or in part, or stored
in a retrieval system, or transmitted in any form or by any means, electronic,
mechanical, photocopying, recording, or otherwise, without written permission of the publisher. For information regarding permission, write to
Little, Brown & Company, Inc., 205 Lexington Avenue, New York, NY
10010.

ISBN 0-590-32196-X

Copyright © 1961 by Scott Corbett. All rights reserved. Published by
Scholastic Inc., 730 Broadway, New York, NY 10003, by arrangement with
Little, Brown & Company, Inc. APPLE PAPERBACKS is a registered
trademark of Scholastic Inc.

12 11 10 9 8 7 6 5 4 3 2 1   7 8 9/8 0 1 2/9

Printed in the U.S.A.   28

First Scholastic printing, August 1987

To Elizabeth
With Love

THE MAILBOX TRICK

1

WHEN THE MAILMAN finally brought his birthday present from Great-aunt Cora, two days late, Kerby Maxwell was not too excited.

Aunt Cora was a nice old lady, but she was one of those people who always give sensible presents nobody wants. Things like three plain white handkerchiefs, or a shoeshine kit, or a set of stiff hairbrushes that hurt, or a dozen monogrammed bookmarks.

"Hurry up and open it, Kerby, I want to see what it is!"

The way his Cousin Gay was jumping up and down and clapping her hands you would have thought it was *her* present. She had to put her nose into everything he did, and she wanted to tag along after him everywhere he went — and Kerby couldn't see why in heck she had to stay with *them* while Uncle Bob and Aunt Martha went on a trip. She was a pest. He couldn't even get on his new bicycle without her wanting him to let her ride on the handle bars. Well, he was darned if he was going to give a girl a ride on his handle bars!

"Oh, be quiet! I'll hurry if I want to!" he growled as he worked the string over one corner of the package.

"Kerby Maxwell, don't you speak to your cousin that way," ordered his mother.

"Well, gee!" growled Kerby.

His mother and Gay and his dog, Waldo, had all gathered around to watch him open the present. It was not a large box. It was not light, but it was not heavy either. It was not much of anything, and not very interesting.

Kerby did not realize just how uninteresting a box could be, however, until he opened this one.

"A box of writing paper!" he cried in horror. Aunt Cora could have thought and thought and not have thought of anything he wanted less. He saw trouble ahead right away, even before his mother made a fuss over the present the way mothers do when they are trying to convince you that a punk present is really very nice.

"Why, it's just what you needed!" she said. "Now you've got your very own stationery to write your thank-you letters on!"

"Look!" cried Gay. "Envelopes and air mail stickers and

even stamps!" As if that were something to be happy about. How could girls be so dumb?

"It's a lovely present," said his mother. "Well, now, you two can go out and play until lunch — but this afternoon why don't you sit down and get your thank-you letters out of the way, Kerby?" she suggested, just as he had feared she would. "You can start by writing one to Aunt Cora on her very own present."

"Do I have to?" groaned Kerby. Usually he was able to put off writing those old thank-you letters for much longer than this. Furthermore, it was hard enough to write them for presents you did like, let alone for presents you did not like. *Dear Aunt Cora, thank you very much for the beautiful white handkerchiefs. I am sure I will get a lot of use out of them every day* — he had written more darn letters like that!

"Come on, Kerby, let's go out and play!" said Gay, tugging at his arm.

He gave her an annoyed look.

"Okay, let's play hide-and-seek and you be It," he snapped.

"No, I don't want to play that again — because when we do, I never can find you."

"Now, Kerby, don't you do one of your disappearing acts,"

warned Mrs. Maxwell. "Take your cousin out and show her around."

"I *have* showed her around — and besides, I want to go over and see Fenton and Bumps, and girls are not allowed in our clubhouse."

"Talk to them outside."

"But our club meets *inside!*"

"Well, if you can't take your cousin along, then you can just wait till later to go to your clubhouse. She's only been here two days, and until Kathy Claypool gets home from camp, Sunday, I want you to look out for her. After that maybe Gay can play with her, some of the time."

"Sunday! That's a long time."

"That's only four days," said Gay.

"Five!" said Kerby, disgusted. "Gee, you can't even count days right!"

Gay checked on her fingers.

"I forgot Thursday," she announced cheerfully.

"Run on outside now, and pretty soon we'll have lunch," said Mrs. Maxwell.

Kerby stalked through the kitchen and out the back door with Gay right on his heels and Waldo right on *her* heels. That was something else Kerby was annoyed about —

Waldo obviously thought Gay was wonderful. He let her put a red ribbon around his neck and everything. It shocked Kerby to find he had a sissy dog!

Directly behind Kerby's back yard was a vacant lot. Bumps Burton lived on one side of it, and Fenton Claypool on the other.

Before the church pageant a couple of weeks ago, Bumps Burton had been a big bully that nobody liked. But then, because the three of them got in trouble together, they ended up by making friends. Before that, Bumps had not let anybody else play in the vacant lot, but now they had built themselves a clubhouse there.

A fence separated Kerby's back yard from the vacant lot, but there was a loose board that could be shoved sideways. Kerby slipped through, and Gay and Waldo slipped through close behind him.

The clubhouse stood in the middle of the lot under a tree. As soon as he stepped through the fence Kerby could see that the club had troubles. The clubhouse was leaning at a dangerous angle, and Bumps and Fenton were busy propping it up with a long board.

"Hey, what happened?" cried Kerby, and ran to join them.

"Aw, we didn't use enough nails!" said Bumps. He was big and strong, but awkward. Fenton Claypool had to keep telling him not to push too hard as they propped up the clubhouse. It was Fenton who thought of bracing the bottom end of the board against the tree, too. Fenton was usually the one who thought of things. He was a tall, thin boy who held himself as straight as a soldier, with his shoulders back, and who usually looked as solemn as an owl. He was the politest boy Kerby had ever known that wasn't a sissy.

"We'd better have a meeting and decide how we're going to fix this," suggested Fenton, and they agreed this was a good idea. Then Kerby remembered his Cousin Gay.

"Aw, I forgot — my mom says I can't leave *her*," he grumbled, jerking his thumb at Gay. She didn't let it bother her, though. Nothing ever seemed to bother her. She just stood there smiling brightly at the boys as though they were all her friends.

As usual, Fenton thought of a plan.

"Why can't she be our mascot, sort of, like Waldo, and stand guard outside to see that nobody comes near while we're having our secret meeting? You want to do that, Gay?"

"Yes, if you don't meet too long," said Gay.

"We'll make it a short meeting," promised Fenton. He

was pretty smart, all right, but then he had a little sister himself. He was used to these problems.

Fenton turned to Bumps.

"What about it, Bumps? Okay? You're president of the club, how about calling a meeting?"

"Okay," said Bumps, "I hereby call a meeting. Let's go."

They crawled inside.

They had to crawl in, because their door was small, more like the door on a doghouse than a real door. The clubhouse was mostly made out of old lumber some workmen had given them from a house that was being torn down in the next block. The clubhouse was big enough for all three of them to be in at once without being crowded. Kerby, who was the shortest, could stand up in it, and even Bumps could almost stand up in it, if he stooped a little. They had cut a small window in one wall and were planning many other improvements, such as a real door, for later on.

"The meeting'll come to order," said Bumps, and they sat down on boxes. "Well, if you ask me, we didn't use enough nails."

"It's more than that, I think," said Fenton. "I think we've got to brace it right."

A suggestion came in through the window.

"Nail the board to the tree!" cried Gay in her high, piping voice.

"Hey!" Frowning angrily, the club president jumped up — which was a mistake. He forgot to stoop. "Ow!" he cried, rubbing his head. "Darn it, she's not supposed to be listening!"

"Hey, get away from here!" cried Kerby, crawling outside to chase Gay away. He shook a finger at her. "Listen, stand guard farther away! This is a secret meeting! Go on, now!"

Reluctantly, Gay moved a couple of feet the other side of the tree.

Waldo moved back too, and sat down beside her.

"Now stay there!" ordered Kerby, and crawled inside again. Bumps was still rubbing his head.

"How long is she gonna be around?" he demanded.

"Three weeks," said Kerby, and they all groaned.

"Well, you got my sympathies," said Bumps. "Now, what were we talking about? Oh, yeah. Fenton thinks we need braces."

"The worst of it is, she's probably right," said Fenton, lowering his voice. "We probably *should* nail the board to the tree."

"I told you so!" cried a piping voice through the window.

12

It was such a shrill, high voice that it made all three of them shoot off their boxes like springs.

"Darn you, Gay!" cried Kerby, scrambling out the door again to *really* chase her away this time. He was mad enough to give her a good push. He probably would have, too, if he hadn't tripped. When he rushed around the corner of the clubhouse he tripped over the board that was bracing it and fell flat on his face.

"Look out, Bumps!" cried Fenton, who had also scrambled quickly out of the clubhouse. Kerby had kicked the board loose. It fell with a clatter, and as it did there was a loud creaking sound. The clubhouse leaned sideways like a tired old man and collapsed in a heap.

With Bumps in it!

When Bumps came crawling out of the wreckage on his hands and knees he was unhurt, but he had not been so mad since the time Kerby made him fall and cut his knee.

"Get out of here! Go on, go home! Beat it! And take her with you!" he yelled at Kerby, pointing at Gay. She was trembling behind the tree, peeking around the side of it with a pale face. "You're out of the club, and if I catch you even coming near the clubhouse again I'll twist your nose so hard you'll — you'll breathe upside down!"

With Bumps Burton in that kind of mood, it was no time

to hang around and argue. Kerby rubbed his aching, bleeding shin and stood up.

"All right, if that's the way you feel!" he retorted, and limped away toward the fence and home. Gay followed at a distance — what she probably decided was a safe distance.

Home in his own yard, Kerby limped to the outside faucet and turned it enough to start a gentle stream flowing through the garden hose. Over near the hedge he picked up the hose and washed the blood off his shin. It stung, too.

Gay stood a good way off and watched him.

"Gee, I'm sorry, Kerby," she said in a tiny voice.

He didn't even say anything. He simply glared at her for a minute over his shoulder. If looks could kill, she would have toppled over exactly like the clubhouse.

"When you're through with the water I'll turn it off for you," she offered, trying to be helpful, and ran over to the faucet.

Kerby dabbed at the cut for a while longer, until it stopped bleeding so much, and then growled, "Okay, turn it off."

Gay gave the faucet a twist. A sharp spurt of water nearly took his leg off.

"You turned it the wrong way!" he yelled, swinging the hose away from his leg.

Unfortunately, he swung it toward a thin place in the hedge. The stream spurted straight through into Mrs. Pembroke's yard next door. There was a loud yowl, and her old cat, Xerxes, leaped about four feet into the air, soaking wet. And in less time than it takes to tell, Mrs. Pembroke came flying out of her kitchen into the yard, breathing fire.

"Yes, ma'am — I didn't mean to — it was an accident," Kerby told her as she bawled him out; but Mrs. Pembroke didn't believe him. He was constantly getting into trouble with her, because she didn't like boys and dogs — only cats.

"And if this happens again I won't go just to your mother, I'll call the *police!*" she finished, and stamped away into her house with Xerxes in her arms, talking baby-talk to him and telling him how she would "dwy" him off "dood wif a nice big towel."

This time, when Kerby looked around, Gay was not even in sight. She had fled into the house. Kerby glowered at Waldo.

"And *you* think she's so great." He sat down on the back steps with his elbows on his knees and his fists jammed against his cheeks. "Three weeks! How am I ever going to stand her for three whole weeks?"

2

AFTER SOAKING Xerxes, Kerby knew it was a cinch he would have to stay in after lunch and work on his thank-you letters.

"I really ought to make you write a note of apology to Mrs. Pembroke, too," said his mother sternly. "If you get into one more bit of trouble with her, I'll make you do more than that. You're to stay off her property and leave her cat alone, do you understand?"

"Yes, Mom."

"Now march up to your room and get started on those thank-you letters. Gay, you can play in your room, or read a book, or do whatever you want to."

"I think I'll read, Aunt Pris," said Gay, and when Kerby went upstairs to his room she followed him up and went to hers. And as usual, Waldo tagged along behind *her,* instead of coming with Kerby.

Kerby sat down at his desk, feeling very sorry for himself.

Then he sighed heavily and looked at his list of people he had to thank:

Uncle Bob and Aunt Martha, for the baseball game. Even though they were on a trip, Mom had an address where they could be reached — wouldn't you know it?

Aunt Helen, for the book.

Grandpa and Grandma Willard, for the freight car to add to his model train.

Grandpa and Grandma Maxwell, for the Ping-pong set.

And Aunt Cora, for the sweet, lovely, darling box of writing paper.

Kerby rose restlessly and crossed the hall to his parents' bedroom. From the windows there, he could look over into the vacant lot. The clubhouse was propped up again. It didn't look too steady, but at least it was all in one piece. Bumps and Fenton were nowhere in sight. Maybe they were inside, holding a secret meeting . . . without him. Sighing again, Kerby returned to his room, shut the door firmly, and sat down again at his desk.

Opening the box, he took out a sheet of paper and drew his long ballpoint pen from its holder like a sword from its scabbard. He chewed on the top end of it for a while, trying to think of what to say about his new baseball game, but all

18

that happened was that he got a funny taste in his mouth from the pen.

Instead of thinking about what to write, he began to think about how everybody was unfair to him. His mother was unfair to him. Mrs. Pembroke was unfair to him. Bumps Burton was unfair to him.

It wasn't fair!

He picked at a fleck of dried paste on a leaflet that had been lying on his desk ever since school ended, and unfolded the leaflet idly. It was an announcement of a Good Citizenship Letter-Writing Contest for school children, sponsored by the Governor of the state. Everybody had been given a copy of the announcement a few days before the end of school; and a few eager beavers like Austin Gilhooley had gone straight to work writing letters. Miss Kingsley had even made Austin read his aloud in class before he mailed it in to the contest.

Kerby could still remember some of the things Austin had written in his letter. Stuff about "our forefathers" and "land of freedom and opportunity," finishing up with "and that is why I am proud to be an American." Austin was a drip, but still Kerby hoped he would win. It would be great for someone from their school to win.

Kerby read part of the announcement, and saw that the contest was already closed. All letters had to be postmarked not later than . . . He looked up at the calendar on his wall.

"Last Thursday," he muttered. Well, he would not have wanted to write a letter for the contest, anyway; but if he *had* wanted to, there were certainly a few things he could have said about Good Citizenship. Take Bumps Burton, now . . .

With his head suddenly full of things to write about, Kerby spread out the blank and, just for fun, started a letter exactly the way it said to.

First he wrote the date. Next he wrote *Governor John Davis Bancroft, State Capitol Building,* and the name of the state capital, and the state. And then he wrote:

Dear Governor Bancroft:

I never did get around to writing you a letter about Good Citizenship when I was still in school. But if you want to know about what Good Citizenship ought to be I can tell you plenty because I am having troubel with a Bad Citizen.

Just because my girl cuzin made me trip over a board and knock down our clubhouse he won't even let me come in our clubhouse any more.

He can do this because he is president of our club and also bigger than me. He can push me out and beat me up if I try

20

to come in. He said if I even come *near* he will twist my nose.

I don't think this is Good Citizenship.

This is the same thing as America. America is like a big clubhouse and everybody that belongs to the club ought to be able to come in to the clubhouse. And big guys should not keep out little guys because they are bigger and are mad at the little guys because they have a girl cuzin that makes them trip over a board and knock down the clubhouse. I think America should be that way.

Very truly yours,
KERBY MAXWELL

When he had finished, he read his letter over and thought it was pretty good. Maybe it wasn't as good as Austin Gilhooley's, but everybody knew Austin Gilhooley was good at writing and always got 100 on almost everything he wrote.

Just for fun Kerby even addressed an envelope to put his letter in. He addressed it to the Governor at the Capitol building in the state capital, exactly the way it said to in the announcement.

While he was doing this, Waldo came padding down the hall and scratched at his door. Kerby let him in, but gave him a dirty look.

"Sissy!" he jeered, but Waldo didn't even hang his head. He just sat down and looked up with his pink tongue hanging out of his mouth, happy as could be.

21

Kerby folded his letter, put it in the envelope, and sealed it. He held it up for Waldo's inspection.

"Just think, all I'd have to do would be to stick a stamp on that and put it in a mailbox and it would go straight to the Governor of the whole state!" he said, for it had suddenly struck him that this *was,* after all, what would happen; and what a wonderful thing it was that even a small boy could write a letter to anybody he wanted to, *if* he wanted to. He had never really thought about it that way before.

The thought gave him a new feeling of power. He even took one of his stamps and pasted it on the letter, just to make it complete, and the simple action made him fairly tingle with this new feeling of power he had.

But then he remembered the contest was over. The Governor would not bother to read Kerby's letter even if Kerby did mail it, which he wasn't going to do anyway. Besides, it was such a crazy letter — all that stuff about Bumps Burton and the clubhouse — that it made Kerby laugh just to think about it.

"Heck, I'd better get started on those darn old thank-you letters," he reminded himself, tossing it aside. "Waldo, you're lucky you're a dog and can't write!"

He tried hard to think what to say about his new baseball game. But instead he kept thinking about the feeling of

23

power that letter had given him. He could write to the Governor if he wanted to — or even the President of the United States! And plenty of other people, too. He could even write to —

Bumps Burton!

The very thought of it made him snicker. What fun it would be to tell off that big bully in a letter! Quickly he took out another piece of paper and began to write:

Mr. Bumps Burton
DEAR SIR:

You are a big loudmouth bully and for 2¢ I would knock your big fat head off.

Very truly yours,
KERBY MAXWELL

In a letter you could write *anything!* So long as you didn't mail it, of course. But it was fun to address an envelope, and stick a stamp on it, and put the letter in it, and seal it, and think what Bumps Burton's face would look like if he ever opened up a letter like that.

Kerby held it up in the air, half-closed his eyes, and let it drop. He was imagining how it would feel to drop it in a mailbox and hear the mailbox bang shut and know it was going straight to Bumps Burton in the next morning's mail.

24

It gave him a big goose-pimply thrill of fright simply to think about it. Why, Bumps would twist his whole head off! In fact, he would do worse than that. But still, think of Bumps's face when he read the letter!

Kerby sat back and laughed and laughed. And while he was still laughing, he thought about Mrs. Pembroke.

"Oh, boy!" said Kerby, and reached for another sheet of paper.

Mrs. Irma Pembroke
Dear Madam:

You ought to shut up about calling the police because if anybody ought to call the police I ought to call the police and tell them to put *you* Y.O.U. in jale because you are an old pain in the neck who are always getting sore about *everything*.

Yours very truly,
Kerby Maxwell

P.S. And that goes for your big fat old cat Yerk . . . Zerkey . . . with the crazy name. You know who I am talking about.

This time Kerby laughed twice as hard. He kept bursting out again and again while he was addressing the envelope and sticking the stamp on it, and he had just put the letter in and sealed it when he heard Gay coming down the hall. He

25

grabbed his letters and shoved them into his desk drawer just before she knocked on his door and came in.

"Don't come in till I say 'Come in!' " he scolded.

"Oh! All right," said Gay brightly, and went out again. She closed the door and knocked.

"Oh, come in!" snapped Kerby. "What do *you* want, anyway?"

"What were you laughing about?"

"Nothing. I was working on my thank-you letters."

"They must be funny ones. Can I read them?"

"No! Go away, I'm busy."

"I don't see any letters."

"I put them away. And now I've got to write another one, so go away and read your book some more."

"Oh, all right, if you won't even show anybody *anything,*" said Gay, pouting, and went back to her room with her head down.

Kerby took out his three letters and started to tear them up, but they were such fun to look at and think about that he hated to do it right away; and besides, the stamps were good and he wanted to soak them off and save them. He put the letters away in his drawer again and went to work on some real ones.

After a while Kerby's mother came upstairs and found him chewing the end of his pen and frowning into space.

"Have you written any letters?"

"Aw, I tried a couple, but they weren't any good."

"Now, don't waste your good stationery on mistakes."

Kerby squirmed guiltily.

"I won't, Mom."

Mrs. Maxwell sighed. "Honestly, Kerby, I never saw anyone have more trouble writing letters! Let them go for now. It's so nice out that you and Gay really should be outside."

"Oh, boy! Can we go out now?"

"*May* we, Kerby."

"Okay, may we?"

"Yes. But I do want those letters written, and soon."

"Sure, Mom!"

"All right, then, you may go out," said his mother, and he didn't realize until too late that she had a wicked twinkle in her eye. She called down the hall to Gay.

"Gay!"

"Yes, Aunt Pris?"

"Dear, would you like to go outside and watch Kerby mow the lawn?"

"Aw, gee whiz, Mom!"

3

EARLY the next morning Fenton Claypool came over to see Kerby. He was his usual solemn, polite self, saying "Good morning, Mrs. Maxwell" and "Thank you, Mrs. Maxwell," when Kerby's mother told him to come in.

Mrs. Maxwell was about to go downtown shopping. She had been giving Kerby and Gay their instructions about what they were to do while she was gone.

"You can play in the yard or go to the park, Kerby, provided Gay goes with you. I don't want you to go off and leave her alone for a minute. You're to take care of your cousin, do you understand?"

"Yes, Mom," sighed Kerby.

"And let me ride on the handle bars," added Gay in her fresh, merry way.

"Nothing doing!"

"I betcha you're not a good enough bike rider to do it!"

"I betcha I am, if I wanted to, only I don't want to!"

"Now, children, that will be enough. You have your instructions. I'll be home in time for lunch."

Mrs. Maxwell turned to Fenton and asked about the clubhouse. Kerby had told his mother and father all about what had happened. Gay had interrupted about a hundred times, of course, wanting to tell about it too.

"Well, Fenton, how's the clubhouse?"

Fenton grinned unexpectedly — on his solemn face, grins were always unexpected.

"Not so good, Mrs. Maxwell. We're still working on it."

"Is Bumps still so mad?"

"Well . . . I'm working on that too."

Mrs. Maxwell laughed.

"Fenton, I think you'll be in the Diplomatic Service when you grow up! Even if you do smooth things over, though, I don't think Kerby had better attend any club meetings this morning, because he'll have to have Gay with him."

"Well, I can't be there, either, today, Mrs. Maxwell. I have to go with my mother to see my grandmother."

Kerby felt like kicking a chair. More bad news! He had hoped maybe Fenton was going to hang around with him and do something. Now he wouldn't have *anybody* to play with.

When his mother had left, Kerby said, "Gee, Fenton, do you *have* to go to your grandma's?" and Fenton said he was afraid he did.

"But I wanted to tell you I think I've got things fixed up with Bumps," he added. "I think that by tomorrow he'll be ready to let you come back into the club."

"Aw, I'm not sure I want to, the big dumb ox!" blustered Kerby. "Just because he's dumb enough to sit inside while the clubhouse falls on top of him . . . You got outside before it fell down, didn't you? Why couldn't he? 'Cause he's a big dope, that's why!"

"He's just a little slow and clumsy. He's not so dumb," protested Fenton. He was always like that — he looked for the best in everybody. "Bumps has a lot of imagination." Fenton chuckled. "Remember the time before the church pageant, when he said he would twist your nose like a doorknob? And yesterday, when he said he'd twist your nose around till you were breathing upside down — I thought that was even funnier!"

"I'm glad *you* thought so," said Kerby bitterly.

"Well, you have to admit it takes some imagination to think up things like that," said Fenton, still enjoying himself.

"Twist it like a doorknob! Gee, that's funny!" whooped Gay.

"Oh, be quiet!" snapped Kerby.

"Well, anyway, I have to get back home again, because we're going to leave soon," said Fenton. "I just wanted to tell you I think I can fix things up with Bumps."

"A doorknob! A doorknob!" chanted Gay, marching around the kitchen with Waldo beside her, looking up at her as if she were the funniest thing he had ever seen. Kerby rolled his eyes sadly in Fenton's direction.

"*You* have a little sister around *all* the time, when she isn't at camp," he said. "How do you stand it?"

Nothing bothered Gay, though. It was impossible to insult her. As soon as Fenton had left she clapped her hands together and cried, "Oh, I know what! Let's play dress-up!"

"*Dress-up!*" echoed Kerby, outraged by the mere suggestion of so childish a game. "*Me* play dress-up? Are you nuts? I haven't played dress-up for so long I can't even remember the last time."

"You dressed up like an angel for the church pageant, Aunt Pris said."

"That was different."

"Why can't we play dress-up inside the house? Nobody will ever know."

"Nothing doing. . . . Look, I got stuff I have to do in my room for a while. Go read a book or something, and pretty

soon we'll go outside, or something," said Kerby, and went up to his room.

Actually he didn't know *what* to do with himself with Gay around. He was almost desperate enough to sit down and write some of those old thank-you letters, for want of something better to do. Plopping down in his chair, he stared at Great-aunt Cora's box of stationery with a dark frown on his face.

After a while, though, he stopped frowning and began to grin as he remembered the letters he had written yesterday — the letter to Bumps and the one to Mrs. Pembroke especially. He decided he had better soak the stamps off them and tear the letters into little bitty pieces, but first he would read them over once, just for laughs. Maybe it would be fun to pretend he was Bumps opening Bumps's letter and reading it, and then pretend he was Mrs. Pembroke reading hers. Pulling his desk drawer open, he reached in for the letters.

They were gone.

Tingling with sudden alarm, Kerby yanked the drawer out completely and scrabbled through its contents with anxious hands as he knelt over it on the floor. Paper, pencils, erasers, crayons, rubber bands, paper clips . . .

But no letters.

Turning to the desk, he peered inside the drawer slot to make sure the letters were not stuck inside somewhere. He was reaching in, feeling around frantically, when Gay came skipping upstairs and poked her head into his room.

"What are you doing, Kerby?"

"My — my letters!" he gasped. "I had some letters —"

"Your letters? Oh, don't worry about them," said Gay brightly. "I took them."

Angry but relieved, Kerby leaped to his feet and seized her roughly by the arm.

"Where are they?"

He looked so fierce that for once Gay was frightened. Her eyes grew round and she looked ready to cry.

"I — I only wanted to do something nice for you," she said, beginning to tremble. "All I did was look in your drawer for an eraser, and I saw you forgot to mail your letters," she explained, "so I ran to the corner with them and mailed them."

4

IF GAY had suddenly hit him over the head with a baseball bat she could not have stunned Kerby more. He stared at her blankly for a moment. Then he staggered to his feet, still staring at her, and sort of toppled into his chair. He looked like somebody who had just been shot on television.

What was he going to do? What would happen when Bumps Burton got his letter? And Mrs. Pembroke hers?

It was too awful to think about.

Meanwhile Gay had begun to cry.

"Kerby, what's the matter? What's the matter? What did I do wrong?"

Though he still felt stunned, Kerby stared at her with what was almost a new respect. You had to hand it to her — anybody who could do anything *this* awful was pretty special. And yet at the same time it was plain that she hadn't done it to be mean, and that she felt bad about doing something wrong even before she knew what was wrong about it.

The crazy part of it all was that he didn't even hate her.

This was the worst disaster of his whole life, and yet he almost felt sorry for her, she looked so little and so miserable.

"When did you mail them?" he asked.

"When I got tired of watching you m-mow the lawn and went inside to draw p-pictures," blubbered Gay, while Waldo looked up at her and whined sympathetically. "I went to look for an eraser in your desk and saw the letters, and I thought maybe you would like me better if I did something nice for you, so I sneaked out of the house with them and ran to the corner and mailed them. And now you don't like me even more than you already didn't!" she finished, sobbing noisily.

All this was embarrassing, of course. And anyway, it wasn't exactly true. Kerby fidgeted in his chair and reassured her gruffly.

"Aw, stop bawling. I like you all right — at least, I don't *not* like you. It's not your fault you're only a girl," he pointed out in all fairness.

But this was no time to sit around talking about who liked who.

"Lookit, I got to do something quick!" he declared.

"But what's *wrong?* Why shouldn't I mail your thank-you letters?"

"Those weren't thank-you letters. Far from it!" groaned

Kerby. "Far, far from it! Didn't you even look at who they were addressed to?"

"It's not polite to look at other people's mail," said Gay primly. "And besides, I couldn't read your writing."

"Well, one of them was to Bumps Burton, and another was to Mrs. Pembroke, and when they read them I'm sunk!"

"Why?"

"Because I told Bumps I'd knock his head off, and I told Mrs. Pembroke she was an old pain in the neck!"

At least this made Gay stop crying. Her mouth fell open. "You didn't!"

"Yes, I did! I was only writing for fun. I never meant to mail them."

"Oh, gosh, Kerby! What *are* you going to do?"

"I don't know!"

Kerby held his head in his hands, hoping that would help. His nose already hurt, just from thinking about what Bumps would do to it. And he could practically feel the policeman's hand on his shoulder when Mrs. Pembroke had him arrested. After all, she had said she would call the police next time.

Fenton Claypool! Maybe Fenton could think of something — But then he remembered. Fenton was gone for the day. Kerby was on his own.

It was a very lonely feeling.

If anybody was going to think of anything, it had to be himself. So Kerby tried to think. After trying hard for a moment and getting nowhere, he looked up at Gay. By now she was perched on the edge of another chair, biting her nails.

"Stop biting your nails, Gay. What time is it?" He hurried across the hall to look at his father's alarm clock. "Nine-thirty! The postman will be coming down Bumps's street any minute now, I think."

He rushed to the window. Over in the vacant lot he could see Bumps working on the clubhouse, putting more nails in it.

"The postman comes down Bumps's block first," Kerby muttered to Gay and Waldo, who had followed him. "He doesn't get to our house until after he goes there. He has to go down a couple of blocks and come back up, and it takes him a while. Fifteen minutes, I guess, maybe more."

All sorts of fantastic plans flashed through Kerby's desperate mind. Maybe he could get Waldo to bite the postman and make him drop his mail before he got to Bumps's house. No, that wasn't any good — Waldo would never do it. He liked the postman. Maybe Gay could pretend to be lost and — No, that wasn't any good either.

Then, as they stood at the window, it was too late anyway.

Here came the postman into sight, leaving Fenton's house and heading for Bumps's.

"Golly! There he is!"

"Oh, Kerby! What are you going to *do?*"

"Quiet! Let me think!" said Kerby, but he couldn't think of a thing. He could only watch helplessly while the mailman walked up onto Bumps's side porch, and Mrs. Burton came to his side door, and the postman handed her the mail.

While Mrs. Burton held open the screen door, he showed her a letter. Kerby gasped. Was it his letter?

Mrs. Burton took the rest of the mail, tossed it on a table beside the door, took some money out of a drawer and gave it to the postman. Kerby realized there must be some postage due on a letter. Well, that couldn't be his, then. His was certainly not very heavy. That meant that his letter to Bumps must be in the bunch of mail Mrs. Burton had tossed on the table . . . And if she would only leave it there, maybe . . .

"Listen, Gay, will you help me do something?"

"Sure, Kerby! What?"

"I'm going to try to get my letter back!"

"Gee! How?"

"We'll sneak over to Bumps's house, and you ring the back doorbell and ask his mother something. And while you're doing that . . ."

"You'll go to the side door and get the letter!"

"Yes!"

"But what'll I ask her?"

"Oh, tell her . . ." Kerby swallowed, and then went on. It was no time to be proud. "Tell her you want to see Bumps. Tell her I sent you over to find out if it was all right for me to come over to the clubhouse yet. Tell her anything, only keep her busy for a minute! Let's go!"

5

A TALL HEDGE ran all the way around Mrs. Pembroke's back yard, and the same kind of tall hedge separated Bumps's yard from the vacant lot. It would screen them from Bumps's view, as long as he stayed over in the lot working on the clubhouse.

But there were plenty of other difficulties.

To stay out of Bumps's sight all the way, they would have to crawl through Mrs. Pembroke's hedge, cut across a corner of her property, and crawl through her back hedge into Bumps's back yard. If Mrs. Pembroke saw them she would rush out and complain so loudly that Bumps would be sure to hear. Not only that, she would tell Kerby's mother, who had specifically warned him to stay off Mrs. Pembroke's property and not get into any more trouble with her — and he knew his mother meant business.

If they crossed Mrs. Pembroke's property without trouble, then they would have to hope Mrs. Burton would not look out and see them coming and wonder what they were doing.

Finally, there was Bumps to worry about. What if he decided to come home for something and caught Kerby sneaking out the side door of *his* house? That was something Kerby tried not to think about as he stood on his own back steps and looked across at Mrs. Pembroke's windows to see whether she was anywhere in sight, or safely out of their way.

"I don't see her," he muttered. "So — come on!"

They left Waldo locked in the house, whining and scratching to get out. He knew he was missing something, but of course Kerby did not dare take him along. They walked down the back steps into their yard, and over to the thin place in the hedge, which was the easiest place to go through.

"Now, follow me. Run across the corner of her yard as fast as you can, and go through the hedge where I do, because I know the best place," said Kerby, and crouched down to go through the first hedge.

He found himself face to face with the cat, Xerxes, who was also crouched down, switching his tail, peering at him with suspicious yellow eyes from the other side.

"Xerxes, get out of the way! I'm not going to hurt your old property," whispered Kerby.

Xerxes answered with a nasty meow. His meow as good as said he didn't believe a word of it.

"Come on, Xerxes, I haven't got time to argue!"

43

But Xerxes sat there switching his tail back and forth, looking suspicious. Kerby decided he would have to try to bluff him.

"Okay, Xerxes, you asked for it!" He turned and made a big show of calling Waldo. "Sic 'em, Waldo!"

Xerxes had heard that phrase often enough to know it. His back went up and he sprang away with a yowl of pleasure toward a tree — he was an excellent tree climber, and he loved it when Waldo gave him a chance to show off.

The instant Xerxes moved, Kerby dived through the hedge, bolted across the corner of Mrs. Pembroke's yard to the other opening, and dived through it into tall grass in the corner of Bumps's yard. Gay came through, too, close behind him — he had to admit she really moved fast, for a girl — and he pushed her down flat in the grass.

"Stay down and don't move!" he hissed — and none too soon. Mrs. Pembroke came bursting out of her back door to find out what was troubling her pet.

"Xerxes! What's the matter? Is someone bothering you?" she asked, and Kerby could imagine how her sharp eyes were darting around in all directions, expecting to see Kerby or Waldo somewhere. It was lucky Bumps didn't keep his lawn mowed clear to the hedge, or the grass would not have hidden them!

44

It was torture, though, having to stay still, waiting for Mrs Pembroke to finish talking baby-talk to Xerxes and go back inside. Those letters were lying on the front hall table in Bumps's house, and any second his mother might take them somewhere else. Kerby could imagine her walking toward them, picking them up . . . Kerby thought Mrs. Pembroke would *never* go back inside; but at last she did.

Now the next thing to worry about was, would Mrs. Burton see them coming? She was probably in the kitchen, and the kitchen was partly shielded by an ell that stuck out from the house on the corner nearest them.

"It's all right if Mrs. Burton sees *you* coming, Gay, so you walk straight to the back door," said Kerby. "I'll go to this side door, and when I hear you talking to her I'll sneak in and grab the letter."

"All right, Kerby." Gay stood up and started walking toward the house. The way she walked — stiff as a doll — he could tell she was scared to death; but she did it, anyway. Even as he was creeping along beside the hedge with his heart in his mouth, Kerby couldn't help but think about that. At least she was not a scaredy-cat! Lots of girls would have whined around and not gone.

When he was opposite the side door he peered through the hedge to make sure Bumps was not coming. Bumps was

still busy, hammering away. Kerby turned around quickl
as he heard Gay knock on the back door.

At first she managed only a timid little knock that Kerb
could hardly hear.

"Louder!" he whispered under his breath. It was all h
could do not to yell it at her in a fury. But then she knocke
again, harder.

He heard steps inside the house and heard Mrs. Burto:
say, "Yes? Who is it?" as she went to the back door. Tw
seconds later he was racing up the steps onto the side porcl
Easing open the screen door, he slipped inside.

Kerby had been in Bumps's house a couple of times be
fore, but *sneaking* in, this way, filled him with a strange an
terrible feeling. It was as if he had never been there before
Everything looked the same, yet nothing seemed familia
The air seemed so thick and still that he could hardly breath
He felt as though everything in sight were frowning at hir
for sneaking in that way. The tall, tall grandfather clock be
side the stairs towered over him menacingly, and seemed t
glare down at him while it whispered: *Tic . . . toc. Tu
. . . tut. Tsk . . . tsk.*

All too clearly, as if she were in the next room — whic
she very nearly was! — Kerby could hear Mrs. Burton talk
ing. She sounded puzzled, but she was being quite nice t

46

Gay. But if she suddenly decided to come here to get something, she could walk into the hall and catch him almost before he could move.

All these impressions went through Kerby's mind in a flash, of course. He didn't waste any time standing around. The mail was still on the table, although Mrs. Burton had opened a couple of the letters and unfolded an advertisement. Kerby's heart leaped when he saw one corner of his letter peeping out of the pile. He grabbed it, stuffed it into his pocket, and turned to go.

From the side porch he could see the vacant lot and Bumps bending over, taking a nail out of a board. Kerby darted down the side porch steps and over to the hedge, and glanced through it. He got a shock.

Bumps had started home for something.

As fast as his legs could carry him, Kerby raced through the yard and dived headlong into the tall grass just two seconds before Bumps came through the hedge not thirty feet away. And one second before Bumps appeared, something dropped into the tall grass so close to Kerby that he nearly jumped out of his skin. It was Gay.

Side by side they lay, still as two field mice, not even daring to breathe, while Bumps clomped past on his big feet. If he even glanced their way he would be sure to see them. . . .

But he didn't. Kerby was ready to burst from holding his breath by the time Bumps disappeared into the back door of the house.

"Whew! That was close!"

"Did you get the letter, Kerby?"

"Yes. Now, if only I could figure some way to get Mrs. Pembroke's from the postman before she does . . ."

It seemed hopeless.

"Shall we sneak across her yard now?"

"Well, let's see where Xerxes is, first."

They were lying in the grass peeping carefully through the hedge when Mrs. Pembroke came to her door and called.

"Come, Xerxes, I want you to come in now," she said — and Xerxes came strolling out from under a bridal-wreath bush, taking his own good time as usual. "I have to go to the store."

As Xerxes slipped inside and Mrs. Pembroke shut the door, Kerby nudged Gay excitedly.

"Did you hear that? She'll be away when the postman comes!"

"What are you going to do?"

"I don't know, but this is my chance. I've got to think of something!"

6

THEY sneaked home safely, across the corner of Mrs. Pembroke's yard, and raced into their house, where Waldo jumped all over them as though they had been gone a week — which, to tell the truth, was about the way it felt to Kerby.

"Look out, Waldo, I want to go watch out the window and see when Mrs. Pembroke leaves," he said, hurrying to the living room. "Stay back from the windows, Gay, so she won't see us."

They waited anxiously.

"Hurry *up,* Mrs. Pembroke, or the postman will come!" Kerby muttered fiercely.

Gay looked up at him and chimed in with, "Yes, hurry up!"

The front door they were watching opened. Out came Mrs. Pembroke, peering into her big black pocketbook and then snapping it shut like a bear-trap.

"There she is! Get back!" whispered Kerby, pushing Gay back so suddenly that she fell over Waldo with a thump that sounded like the whole house falling down. Waldo yelped and Gay said, "Ow!" and Kerby shushed them both. Carefully he peeked through a curtain. "She's looking this way! *Ssh!*"

After glancing toward their house, Mrs. Pembroke turned and craned her neck down the street in the other direction.

"She's looking to see if the postman's coming, I bet," whispered Kerby. "If he comes around the corner now, I'm sunk. She'll wait to see if she has any mail."

But the postman didn't come into sight, and Mrs. Pembroke decided to go on. She walked away, past Kerby's house, and on up the street.

"Now then!" Kerby turned away from the window with a plan already in mind. The minute Mrs. Pembroke opened her door, the mail slot in it reminded him how her mail was delivered. After that he knew there was only one way out of the fix he was in.

When he looked around, he saw that Gay was rubbing her head and that she had tears in her eyes.

"I didn't mean to push you over," he said. "Did you bump your head?"

"My elbow too. But I didn't cry!" she pointed out proudly.

"You're sure not a crybaby," Kerby admitted, and that seemed to make her feel much better. "Come on — I've got to take a look at something!" he said, and rushed through

51

the house with Gay and Waldo close behind. He hurried across the yard, ducked through the hedge, and knelt in front of one of Mrs. Pembroke's basement windows. It was a small window, the kind that swings in on hinges. He was almost afraid to touch it, for fear it might be locked.

"If this is locked, I'm *really* sunk, because she always locks her doors," he said. "She leaves this window open for Xerxes, most of the time, though. Maybe it won't be latched."

Gay, who was on her knees beside him, stared up into his face.

"Kerby! What are you going to do?"

"I've got to sneak into her house and be waiting inside when the postman sticks the mail through the door."

Gay looked terrified.

"Golly, Kerby! That's dangerous!"

"I know. I could even be sent to jail," said Kerby, looking away shamefaced. He knew he was doing something that was against the law, and that if he were caught everybody would call him a regular juvenile delinquent, which would disgrace his family.

His mother had forbidden him to so much as set foot on Mrs. Pembroke's property — which he had already done, and was now doing again. But what would she say if she knew he was trying to *break into* Mrs. Pembroke's *house?* What would his father say?

"But I'm not going to steal anything, I'm just going to take back my own letter," he protested to Gay. "And if I *don't* get it back I'll be in trouble almost as bad as jail!"

They stared at each other for a moment. Then Gay reached out gingerly and gave the window a push.

It swung in. It wasn't locked.

"Oh, boy!" breathed Kerby. He glanced around. Mrs. Pembroke's tall hedge hid them from the other houses. Opening the window, he peeped over the ledge. Below him were two big galvanized-iron sinks.

"Hold the window up for me," he told Gay. A moment later Kerby had backed in through the window, balanced on the edge of the sinks, and jumped to the floor. In another moment he had hurried across the basement and up the stairs. Cautiously he pushed the door open and entered Mrs. Pembroke's kitchen.

Being in Bumps's house had seemed strange and scary. Being in Mrs. Pembroke's was ten times worse. For one thing, he had never been inside her house before. Everything looked shiny and polished and fussy, and again the air had that thick, strangling feeling about it, so that he could scarcely breathe, and there was not a sound except for the ticking of a clock.

This time the clock did not have a slow, solemn tick like the grandfather's clock at Bumps's, though. Here the small wall clock was more like Mrs. Pembroke herself — fussy and sharp and in a hurry: *Tick-quick tick-quick, tick-quick tick-quick,* with a small pendulum flying back and forth furiously. As he tiptoed along the hall past the dining room and into the living room, the scolding tone of the clock made Kerby more nervous than ever.

"Yeow — *ffffffffft!*"

He nearly jumped out of his sneakers. From a large, fluffy basket beside the fireplace, two yellow eyes were glaring balefully. He had forgotten about Xerxes.

"Cut that out, will you?" he replied, glaring back. "Nobody's going to bother you, so shut up!"

But Xerxes wouldn't shut up. He ran through his entire repertoire of meows, growls, snarls, and spits before he finally stopped; and even then he continued to make an occasional threatening remark deep in his throat — while all the time Kerby crouched by the front door, waiting, wishing that the postman would hurry up and come.

Then his heart leaped. The honest tread Kerby knew so

well boomed on the hollow wooden steps outside. Footsteps scuffed across the porch and stopped. Kerby could hear the postman whistling under his breath and envelopes rustling in his hand as he sorted out Mrs. Pembroke's mail. A rectangle of light flashed through the door as he lifted the mail-slot cover, and a bunch of letters pushed their heads through the slot. . . .

New footsteps . . . voices! The postman saying: "Well, good morning, Mrs. Pembroke, you came just in time. Here, I'll save you picking up all this mail off the floor. . . ."

In the midst of the letters Kerby could see the corner of an envelope that looked like his, but there was no time to make sure. With thumb and forefinger he plucked at it desperately and drew it through the slot as the postman pulled the rest of the mail out again.

Holding his breath, Kerby looked at the letter . . .

It was his!

As he scuttled down the hall, keeping low so that Mrs. Pembroke would not see him through the small glass pane in the top part of the door, she thrust her key in the lock. With her so near, and the basement door so far away, Kerby lost his head. His only impulse was to get out of sight, to hide somewhere, anywhere — and a closet door was invitingly ajar. Almost before he knew what he was doing, he had dived inside — tugging the door closed behind him.

The instant he was inside he regretted it. He felt exactly like a mouse who had walked into a trap. He heard the front door open, and pawed around him in the suffocating darkness for something to hide behind. He felt some clothes hanging down around him and realized he was in a clothes closet. A clothes closet! What had Mrs. Pembroke been wearing? Was she wearing a coat she would want to hang up? Kerby could not even remember. All he could hope was that she would have to go upstairs for something, so that he would have a chance to get away.

Mrs. Pembroke's quick footsteps clicked down the hall, and of course she talked baby-talk to Xerxes all the way. Kerby could hear her set down a bag of groceries on the kitchen table and open the refrigerator door.

"*M-r-r-r-r-ow-w.*"

Kerby gasped. Xerxes sounded as if he were right outside the closet door!

"*M-r-r-r-r-r-ow-w-w?*"

He *was!*

"What's the matter, Xerxes?" asked Mrs. Pembroke, coming back from the kitchen. "Now, don't tell Muvver there's a nassy old mouse in the closet? Well, we'll just see . . ."

Her hand was on the doorknob and Kerby's heart was in his mouth when — the doorbell rang.

"Oh, now, who can that be?" asked Mrs. Pembroke, and her quick steps clicked up the hall.

The instant he heard her open the front door Kerby pushed sharply against the closet door and rushed out to escape. As the door gave, there was a mushy thump and a muffled yowl. Sneaking on tiptoe into the kitchen, Kerby looked back and was startled to see Xerxes come staggering away from the hall closet door, shaking his head.

Down the basement stairs sped Kerby, and he was as silent as an Indian on all but one of them — the last one. He stumbled on that one. Stumbled, fell down — and knocked over a basket full of empty tin cans.

The racket they made was unquestionably the worst noise Mrs. Pembroke had heard around her house since last Halloween.

"Oh, golly!" muttered Kerby, and struggled to his feet. He had never climbed anything as fast as he climbed the sinks and the wall to the window. And even then, by the time he was halfway through the window Mrs. Pembroke was looking down from the top of the stairs, unable to see him but certainly hearing him. Luckily she was too frightened to come down.

"Who's down there? Help! Who is that? Poli-i-i-ice!" she screamed, and went rushing away through the house to call for help.

Gay was there to hold the window up for him. He scrambled out and they shot through the hedge and up their back steps into Kerby's house. Kerby darted through the house to the living room windows in time to see Mrs. Pembroke yelling into the ear of a taxicab driver, who was talking on his two-way radio. She had already collected quite a crowd.

"Gosh all hemlock!" said Kerby, awed. "Look at what we started!"

But Gay was looking at Kerby.

"Kerby, your leg's all bloody!"

He glanced down. "Darn it, I must have hit that cut and made it bleed again."

Then a terrible thought struck him like a fist.

"Oh, my gosh! Maybe I left a trailablood!" he cried. That was exactly the way he said "trail of blood," as though it were one word. "Gay, we've got to go see if there's a trailablood out in the yard! Oh, but I can't go out like this!"

"I'll go! You wash your leg off."

While Kerby hastily washed his leg at the kitchen sink Gay ran outside. She was back in a moment, beaming.

"There's not any trailablood in *our* yard!" she announced. "I even peeked through the hedge and I couldn't see any over there either!"

"Good! But maybe there's some bloody stains on whatever I scraped my leg on down in the basement," Kerby pointed out worriedly. "One thing is sure, I can't let anybody see my leg, just in case."

He rushed back to the living room windows in time to see a terrifying sight. A police car had pulled up out in front of Mrs. Pembroke's house, and two huge policemen were jumping out. The way they appeared to Kerby they were both seven feet tall if they were an inch, and every inch of them looked fierce. One ran around to the back yard while the other stayed in front listening to Mrs. Pembroke, who was talking a mile a minute.

Kerby looked down at his leg again — his horrible, telltale leg.

"I can't keep wearing my shorts!" He groaned. "But, if I change and put on long pants, Mom'll want to know why."

Gay stared up at him, and clapped her hands together.

"We'll play dress-up!"

Kerby's mouth fell open. It was amazing that any girl could be so smart!

"Gay, I got to hand it to you," he said generously. "You sure do think of things sometimes. Come on, let's go put on some costumes — anything, so long as mine has long pants!"

7

THEN Gay had another of her ideas. This time she was so pleased she jumped up and down.

"I know! Put on your angel costume!"

"What? Heck, no!"

"But that long robe will cover up your leg best of all."

Against his will, Kerby could not help seeing certain advantages in Gay's idea. If the police did come over to ask questions and found him dressed up in an angel costume, they certainly would not suspect him of being a burglar. Angels did not go around climbing through people's basement windows.

"If the police come they'll think I'm a real goody-goody, playing dress-up in an angel costume with my little girl cousin!" he snorted. It was a humiliating situation to picture, but at the same time he was forced to admit it would be a big help if they *did* think that. He peeked out the window and saw the policemen talking together and glancing around.

The sight helped him make up his mind.

"Come on, quick!"

Kerby's mother had packed away his costume carefully after the pageant. Everything was in a chest — the white robe, the new halo and wings that had to be made after he wrecked the first set, and even his wand.

"I'll put on just the robe," he said, but Gay wouldn't hear of it.

"Put it all on. You want to look as good as you can, don't you? The gooder the better!"

"Oh, all right!" growled Kerby. "I don't feel like arguing."

Gay put on some things Kerby's mother had given her to use for dress-up — a fancy dress and hat, and some white high-heeled shoes. When they were both dressed, and Kerby had allowed Gay to hobble around in her high-heeled shoes and admire his silly old angel costume from all angles, they went downstairs again. Gay had to carry the shoes down, because she could not walk downstairs in them. As for Kerby, he felt foolish with his wings flapping behind him and his halo bobbing around on its stick, but he felt safer.

By now the policemen were nowhere to be seen, but there was a station wagon parked out in front of Mrs. Pembroke's, and a sign on the door said: SHADY HILL DOG AND CAT HOS-

PITAL. DR. C. W. WILKINS, VETERINARY. Soon a man carrying a small black bag came out of the house. Mrs. Pembroke followed him onto the porch.

"I'm sure Xerxes will be perfectly all right, Mrs. Pembroke," the doctor was saying. "He simply got a good bump in the face. His nose will be tender for a day or two, but that's all."

Wide-eyed, Gay turned and whispered a question to Kerby.

"What happened to Xerxes?"

Kerby told her. She giggled.

"Poor Xerxes! First you squirt him and then you bang him on the nose!"

"Well, he got nosy once too often!" said Kerby, but even so he was glad Xerxes was not hurt badly. Later on they saw him out in the front yard. He had some medicine on his nose, but otherwise he looked all right.

After a while Kerby's mother came home from shopping. She was pleased to see Kerby wearing his costume.

"So you put it on for your cousin after all! That's very nice of you, Kerby."

"Huh!" said Kerby, thinking, She should know the half of it!

"He looks wonderful," said Gay. "He's the funniest angel I ever saw!"

"Huh!" said Kerby, frowning at his cousin.

He took off his wings and halo for lunch, but afterwards his mother wanted to take a picture of the cousins together in their dress-up costumes.

"Put everything on and come out in the back yard," she said.

"Aw, I don't want to go outside in this old outfit!" complained Kerby. He would not have wanted to anyway, but this time it was more than that, of course. He was afraid that if he set foot out of doors a policeman would pounce on him. He felt so guilty that he was sure any policeman would only have to take one look at him to know his secret, costume or no costume.

But there was no getting out of the picture.

"Oh, don't be silly," said his mother, "nobody else will see you. Hurry up, now."

"Can I put a big red bow on Waldo so he can be in the picture too, Aunt Pris?" asked Gay. "Can I, Kerby?"

"That's up to Waldo," snapped Kerby. He refused to take any responsibility for the way Waldo was acting lately.

Kerby and Gay posed in the back yard with Waldo sitting between them wearing a huge red bow and looking so

pleased with himself it was sickening. Mrs. Maxwell was bending over her camera, lining up the picture, when around the corner of the house behind her came walking the biggest policeman Kerby had ever seen anywhere! Not just an ordinary policeman, either. A special one with riding pants and a big, wide-brimmed hat.

"This sunlight is too strong, or something," grumbled Mrs. Maxwell, peering through her picture-finder. "Both you children look as white as sheets."

Kerby was too frightened to speak. He knew the end had come. He never should have stepped foot out of the house where they could nab him. He should have stayed inside, forever and ever! Now his father and mother would find out all the terrible things he had done, and he would go to jail for the rest of his life, and . . .

"Pardon me, ma'am," said the policeman in a loud, deep voice that made Kerby's mother jump. "Are you Mrs. Maxwell?"

"Oh! Why — why, yes, I am!" she replied, flustered.

"Excuse me, ma'am, I didn't mean to startle you," said the policeman in his booming voice. He stared at Kerby. "And is that young Kerby?"

"Why, yes!"

"That's quite an outfit. He looks like a real Good Citizen, all right."

He reached inside his coat and drew forth an official document.

"I'm Sergeant McHugh of the state police, attached to the Governor's staff, ma'am," he said, "and I've just driven over from the Capitol with this special invitation for Kerby Maxwell. Here you are, Kerby."

8

MRS. MAXWELL gasped.

"Sp-pecial invit-tation?" she stammered. "What for?"

"Well, Kerby's letter came in too late to win any regular prize in the Good Citizenship Contest, but it was so — well — so *different* that it went through the Capitol like wildfire, and the Governor wants to give Kerby a special award tomorrow for the Most Original Letter," explained Sergeant McHugh.

Mrs. Maxwell whirled to stare at Kerby, who was standing in a trance holding the Governor's special invitation. It was fluttering in his hand like a bird, and under his robe his legs felt like two strands of overcooked spaghetti.

"I gotta sit down," he muttered, and dropped onto the garden bench with a thump.

A man wearing his hat on the back of his head and carrying a big camera on a shoulder strap came around the corner of the house.

"Find 'em, Mac?" he asked, and hurried forward with a

gleam in his eye as he saw Kerby and Gay and Waldo. "Hey, man! Is this the kid? Great! Let me get a shot of this!"

Before Kerby knew what was happening the man was taking their picture.

"A Good Citizen in an angel costume — my editor will eat this up!" exulted the photographer.

"Will this be in the newspaper?" asked Mrs. Maxwell.

"It sure will, lady!"

"Oh, won't that be wonderful!"

Wonderful — in his angel costume, for Pete's sake!

"But, Kerby," she said, "tell me what this is all about."

So he had to explain, very carefully. And this time Gay didn't say a thing, for fear of saying the wrong thing. She knew how careful he would have to be in explaining, so as not to explain *too* much, and she was smart enough to keep still. Kerby only had to look at her once to know she understood.

". . . so I got to thinking about that letter contest, and I wrote a letter to the Governor just for fun, and put a stamp on it and everything, and then Gay saw it and mailed it," he told them as he finished his story.

"It's a pretty funny letter," grinned Sergeant McHugh. "I read it myself."

The invitation was for Kerby to attend the Good Citizenship Day ceremonies at the Capitol building the next day. He was to be on the stand with the governor and all the other important people, including the children who had won the first and second prizes in the contest.

After Sergeant McHugh and the newspaper photographer had left, Mrs. Maxwell hurried inside and telephoned Kerby's father, and Mrs. Maxwell said he would make arrangements right away to take the day off so that they could all drive to the state capital for the ceremonies.

While his mother was on the telephone Kerby and Gay had a chance to talk about what had happened. Gay was wildly excited, but Kerby had a funny feeling about it all. He did not even know yet what it was that bothered him, but something kept him from feeling excited and happy.

"Now aren't you glad I mailed those let — that letter, Kerby?"

"I guess so."

"But isn't it wonderful?"

"Well, it beats being arrested," Kerby was willing to admit, but otherwise he could not seem to feel right about what had happened.

Before long his father came rushing home, and walked around in the house with his chest pushed out saying, "That's my boy!" And then the evening paper came with the picture of Kerby and Gay and Waldo in it, and after that everybody that his mother hadn't already called up called them up to talk about how wonderful it was.

Good Citizen Dresses the Part, said the caption above the picture. Kerby groaned when he read it. There he stood with a scared look on his face and those silly wings on his shoulders and that dopey halo over his head on a stick.

"How am I ever going to live this down?" he groaned.

"But you wore it in the pageant," Gay pointed out. "And you had your picture taken in it then."

"That was different. All the other guys were in that one." Kerby glowered at Gay. "You and your old dress-up! Now look what you got me into! Darn it, I'm going to take off this old robe!"

His parents were busy taking turns on the telephone. He strode away toward the stairs with Gay trotting after him whispering wildly.

"But you can't! They'll see —"

"Never mind!"

Waldo tore himself away from the newspaper picture, which he had been sniffing, and came along. When they were upstairs Kerby hauled up his robe and they all took a look at his leg.

"You see? It's scabbed over now like yesterday. They won't notice any difference. Come on, help me off with my wings."

Kerby took off his wings and halo and robe and looked like his old self again. But he didn't feel like his old self. Something was still bothering him, and he was beginning to understand what it was.

That night they had a special dinner, with steak and French-fried potatoes and *no salad* and peppermint ice cream with chocolate sauce for dessert — all the things Kirby liked best. And the more they all made over him, the worse he felt. When his mother smiled at him proudly he felt like two cents. When his father patted him on the shoulder Kerby seemed to burn and sting all over.

After supper they went to an early movie to settle everybody's nerves, as his mother put it. When they reached home she said, "Well, it's been a big day for both you children and I think you're tired, and tomorrow will be an even bigger day, so you'll want to be rested up for it. You'd better both go to bed now and get a good night's sleep."

Kerby was glad of a chance to get away and be alone. As he and Gay went upstairs he could hear his mother murmuring to his father, "I think he really is exhausted. You notice he went up without a word."

Exhausted or not, he was certainly in no condition to go to sleep. When he had climbed into bed he lay in the dark staring up at the dim rectangle of the ceiling, and he might as well have been lying on a bed of nails. Waldo padded in quietly and lay down on the rug beside his bed, making him feel humbler than ever. That was Waldo every time; when a fellow really needed a friend he was right there.

"Waldo, I take it all back," Kerby apologized, and Waldo looked up at him forgivingly.

By now the trouble was crystal-clear in Kerby's mind.

The trouble was that he was a big phony.

Here he was, supposed to be a Good Citizen who was going to get a Special Award for the Most Original Letter, and what was he really? Not only had he lied to his mother, not only had he disobeyed her special rules, but he was also a plain and simple criminal; and not only that — a criminal who was wanted by the police, if they only knew it.

But what could he do? If he said anything now, he would disgrace his family worse than ever. So far as he could see there was nothing to do but go through with it and get his old award. But if there was anything worse than getting an award you knew you didn't deserve he would like to hear what it could be!

There was a scratch at his door.

"Come in, boy," he said automatically.

"It's me," whispered Gay, and came tiptoeing in.

"Oh, I forgot — Waldo's here," said Kerby, while Waldo's tail, thumping a welcome on the floor, announced his presence. Gay sat down beside Waldo and put her arm around his neck. Kerby could just barely see her. She had on her pajamas and bathrobe and slippers, and looked tinier than ever. She peered up worriedly at Kerby through the dark.

"I'm not sleepy."

"Neither am I."

Something that sounded like a sob came from Gay's direction, and Kerby could hear Waldo's tongue consoling her.

"Kerby, I'm sorry!"

Kerby gulped.

"Aw forget it," he ordered sternly. "It's not your fault. Not all of it, anyway. It's . . . well, it's . . . just the way things happen," he said, struggling to put into words something that was hard to explain. "Don't worry about it. I'll figure things out somehow."

Darn it, though, why did Fenton Claypool have to be away at a time like this? It was very lonely and frightening, having to work out something like this all alone.

9

WHEN MORNING CAME, Kerby still had not thought of anything to do.

There simply was nothing he *could* do, it seemed, but take the award and keep still. With a numb feeling he went through the motions of eating breakfast and getting ready — and his parents decided he was suffering from stage fright.

"Now, don't you worry, son. You won't have to do anything up there on the platform except take your award and shake hands with the Governor," said his father. "You won't have to read your own letter or anything like that."

If he had not felt so terrible Kerby could have laughed at their crazy ideas. Stage fright! That was good. He had lots more important things to worry about than shaking hands with any old Governor on a platform! *That* part didn't bother him at all. If only he didn't have his *real* worries to think about, he could snap his fingers at the rest of it!

"I wish you could remember more about what you said in

your letter," declared his mother. "But still, it will be fun to be surprised."

That was something else Kerby could not be bothered about — trying to remember all the stuff he had said in his letter. With the other things he had on his mind, it just didn't seem important.

When everybody was ready, the five of them drove to the state capital (naturally, Waldo went too). It was a long drive, and the closer they got to the capital the worse Kerby felt.

His parents kept talking about how he should not be nervous.

"And, Gay, I certainly don't see why *you* should be nervous, dear," said Mrs. Maxwell. "Yet you've been as quiet as Kerby all the way. I suppose it's just sympathetic nervousness."

"Might as well admit it, Pris," said Mr. Maxwell with a grin, "you're nervous yourself."

"A fine thing to say, when I'm trying so hard to set a good example!" scolded Mrs. Maxwell. "For that matter, I didn't notice you sleeping much last night."

"Don't be silly. I leapt like a slam. I mean, I slept like a lamb. And I'm as cuke as a coolcumber."

Even Kerby had to laugh at his father's silly talk, but at

the same time it made him unhappier than ever. The worst part of it all was seeing his parents so happy, and he wished everything were really the way they thought it was.

When they reached the state capital they had to leave Waldo in the car while the rest of them went into the Capitol building, but fortunately the ceremonies were going to be held on the lawn outside, and Waldo would be able to attend those. A large platform draped with bunting and flags was already set up on the lawn, with row upon row of chairs lined up in front of it. Men were unloading still more from a truck. The chairs banged cheerfully as the men unfolded them and set them up in rows, and on the platform another man was saying, "One, two, three," into a microphone, testing the public-address system. The sunshine was warm and bright, without being too warm.

"A perfect day!" said Kerby's mother, and once again he winced.

They walked inside the Capitol, where their footsteps echoed hollowly on the marble floors under the great round dome. When they peered up at the towering hollow of the dome, it was so huge and so high above them that it gave Gay goose pimples to look up at it, or at least she said it did. Mr. Maxwell asked a man at an information desk where they should go, and the man told them to wait where they were. A moment later, who should show up but Sergeant McHugh himself!

"The Governor wants to meet you privately before the luncheon starts," he told them. That was another thing — they were even going to have lunch at the Capitol.

Sergeant McHugh took them up the curving marble stairs and along a wide marble hall to the big doors with THE GOVERNOR'S OFFICE printed on them. When they walked in, a secretary greeted them. She went through still another door into the Governor's private office, and told him they were there. In a moment she returned and asked them to go in.

Governor Bancroft stood up from behind his desk and came forward to shake hands. He was a tall man with gray hair and large deep-set eyes. He looked very distinguished. If Kerby had been picking a governor, Governor Bancroft was exactly the kind of man he would have picked.

Another tall man, who was bald and wore glasses and was about as dignified as anybody Kerby had ever seen, also shook hands with them. When Kerby found out who this man was, he had his worst moment yet.

What worse thing could happen to a criminal than to find himself, as he was, shaking hands with the Chief Justice of the State Supreme Court?

"So you're Kerby Maxwell!" said Governor Bancroft when

they had all sat down. "Well, Kerby, I can't tell you how much I enjoyed your letter. And I guess Justice Harrington feels the same way."

"I certainly do," said the great judge, smiling down at Kerby from what seemed to him like a stupendous height. "You had a highly original way of putting your case, Kerby, but nevertheless what you wrote said a lot about America, justice, and equality."

"You really spoke up the way a Good Citizen should, my boy," said Governor Bancroft, "and I wish we had more like you."

At first Kerby was dazed by all this talk, but all of a sudden things stopped swimming in front of his eyes and he saw everything in a cold, clear light — and he couldn't stand it any longer. Something powerful inside him was at work, and though he tried with all his might and main he could not hold it back. He almost felt like two people — one looking on in horror, while the other jumped to his feet and burst out in a loud, shaky voice:

"But I'm not a Good Citizen!"

Governor Bancroft and Justice Harrington reared back in their chairs as though a cherry bomb had gone off under their noses. They exchanged a startled glance.

Kerby's father was the first to find his voice.

"Son! What do you mean?"

After his first outburst, Kerby himself was so startled that he could not reply.

The Governor recovered first, and took a deep breath. When he spoke, his voice was deep and calm.

"My boy, are you trying to tell us you didn't write that letter?"

"No!" said Kerby bitterly. "I wrote the letter, all right. . . ."

"Ah!" said the Governor, and he sat back, looking relieved — terribly relieved. "Well, then, I'm sure you're exaggerating."

"No, sir, honest I'm not. I — I . . ."

Kerby glanced around desperately at his father, his mother, and Gay. Gay's eyes were enormous. When she saw the struggle Kerby was having, she tried to help. Her piping voice made them all jump again.

"Kerby didn't do anything really bad," she announced, "he only snuck into a couple of people's houses!"

"WHAT?" cried everybody, and Governor Bancroft pulled out his breast-pocket handkerchief and patted his forehead with it quite a few times, all over.

"Well, he didn't take anything but his own letters," Gay added.

84

"Kerby! What letters? Whose houses?" thundered his father.

Kerby swallowed.

"Bumps's and Mrs. Pembroke's," he replied in a small voice.

His father had jumped up. Now he sat down again.

"Good grief!" he croaked.

The Chief Justice was more used to handling situations like this than were the rest of them. It was he who finally made a sensible suggestion.

"Kerby," he said, in grave but soothing tones, "I think the best thing would be if you would sit down, calmly and quietly, and tell us all about this, from the beginning."

"That's right, Kerby," urged Governor Bancroft. "Just tell us."

Mr. Maxwell laid his hand on Kerby's shoulder.

"Go ahead, son. Don't be afraid."

Kerby looked at his father, and he was not afraid. He poured out his story. Getting it off his chest was the best feeling he had experienced in a long, long time. No matter what they might do to him, it was a relief to own up.

When Kerby got to the part about Xerxes and Mrs. Pembroke, Governor Bancroft began to develop a bad cough. He kept pulling out his handkerchief and covering his face with it while he wheezed into it. As for Justice Harrington, he hardly moved the whole time, except that now and then he raised one hand and sort of dragged it down across his face. But nobody said a word. Not even Gay. They listened.

When he had finished, there was a long silence. His father looked at his mother. Governor Bancroft looked at Judge Harrington. Judge Harrington looked at Kerby's father. Then everybody looked at Governor Bancroft, because he had cleared his throat. He put the tips of his fingers together and leaned forward.

"Well, Kerby," he said, "I agree that you did some things that you shouldn't have; and I agree that this is a matter for the law. I think I will refer this case to the Chief Justice, and, if you'll excuse us, I'd like to confer with him for a moment privately. If you will all stay here, please, Justice Harrington and I will step into the outer office."

10

WHEN THE DOOR had closed behind them, Kerby turned his pale face toward his father.

"Gee, Dad, what will they do to me?"

His father looked at him gravely.

"I don't know, son; but whatever they decide, I'm sure it will be fair."

"That's what I'm afraid of!" groaned Kerby.

The door opened again. They all stood up. The Governor and the Chief Justice walked to their places, and they all sat down.

Again, Justice Harrington seemed to look down at Kerby from an immense height.

"Now then, Kerby. For entering other people's houses the way you did, you could be arrested and sent to jail, even if you had taken nothing. However, you did take something that did not belong to you. Once Gay had dropped your letter into the mailbox, it was no longer yours. You understand that, don't you?"

Kerby nodded miserably.

"Yes, sir."

"Good. Now, at Bumps's house you committed a crime which the local police could deal with, since the mail had already been delivered. But in taking a letter out of a pack of mail that was still in the postman's hand, as you did at Mrs. Pembroke's, you stole property that was still in the custody of the United States Government, and I suppose we really should turn you over to the Federal authorities. But we will not do that. You see, Kerby, in our courts the spirit of the law is even more important than the letter of the law, and I am confident that not only the postal authorities but such law enforcers as Mr. J. Edgar Hoover and all the other Federal Bureau of Investigation men would agree with me in this case."

"Ulp!" gulped Kerby. The mere thought of having the F.B.I. on his trail was enough to scare the life out of him!

"Taking other people's mail, then, is a serious offense, Kerby," Justice Harrington continued, "but writing the letter to your neighbor Mrs. Pembroke was almost a worse offense, because when you did that you took a chance of hurting another person's feelings very deeply, and unjustly. I will pass over the letter to Bumps Burton — I don't think it would have caused him any pain, though it might have caused *you* considerable. But in the case of Mrs. Pembroke you were being unfair. Accident or not, you *had* soaked her cat with your garden hose. Furthermore, I suspect you and your dog Waldo of having given her a good deal of trouble in the past, and not always by accident. Am I right?"

Kerby hung his head.

"Yes, sir."

Judge Harrington nodded.

"Very well, then. She had a just complaint."

But now the expression on the face of the Chief Justice became less severe and even more wise.

"At the same time, Kerby, I don't propose that you should go next door when you return home and confess to Mrs. Pembroke, because the Mrs. Pembrokes of this world are not always a forgiving lot, but are more inclined to take delight in demanding that the letter of the law be observed. Therefore, with the Governor's backing, I am going to take this case into my own hands and leave Mrs. Pembroke in blissful ignorance of the identity of her burglar. There are times when I am a firm believer that we should let sleeping — er — cats lie, so to speak, and this is one of them. We will pass sentence on you here and now in this room, then, and I will expect you to see to it that your own sentence is carried out. Stand up, Kerby."

Like many another pale prisoner at the bar before him,

Kerby Maxwell stood on trembling legs before his judge. And few of them ever received a greater surprise than did he.

"How many thank-you letters did you say you were supposed to write?"

Kerby stared at the Chief Justice blankly.

"F-five, sir."

"Five. And it was really those five letters that started all this trouble, wasn't it? Therefore, this is your sentence, Kerby. *Within twenty-four hours of the time you reach home you are to write those five letters and get them off in the mail.* They are not to be skimpy ones, either; each is to be at least one full page in length. And you are to sit yourself down and write them without your father or mother or Gay or Waldo having to remind you. Is that clear?"

By now a puny smile was managing to flicker fitfully on Kerby's face.

"Yes, sir!"

"Very well, then. And now that you've given us all the evidence, Kerby, I want to say that in spite of your past crimes I still feel you have the makings of a Good Citizen. I for one will certainly not be ashamed to walk out onto the platform with you."

"Nor will I," said Governor Bancroft.

And that was the moment Kerby's mother picked to start crying. She hugged him, and his father hugged him, and Gay hugged him, and it was as if somebody had rolled a huge stone off his back and he was suddenly as light as a feather. All the grownups started laughing and talking and shaking hands, and Kerby's father told the Governor they had voted for him, and Governor Bancroft said he appreciated it.

Then Governor Bancroft said something about how many thousand people were expected to be on hand to watch the ceremonies.

Mrs. Maxwell was the first to notice that Kerby had suffered a relapse. She was the first to notice that he was pale and a-tremble again.

"For heaven's sake, Kerby, what is it now?"

She took a closer look at him — and burst out laughing. "Wouldn't you know it? Now he's got stage fright!"

Once he was out on the platform with all the others, it was not so bad. When they came to his letter, Governor Bancroft himself read it aloud, as he had the first-prize letter. Kerby was so excited at that point that he hardly heard it at all. He was too busy watching his parents and Gay in the front row, with Waldo on his leash sitting beside them importantly, and looking up as though he, too, understood what a wonderful thing was happening. It was so great to see his parents looking proud, and to know it was all right now for them to *be* proud, that he could hardly take his eyes off them. And when everybody, all those thousands of people, clapped at the end of his letter, and he had to stand up and receive his Special Award and take a bow, that was fun. It made him feel good. When he saw what his award was — a Good Citizenship Certificate, suitable for framing, and a check for fifty dollars — he felt even better.

As soon as they were alone in the car on the way home, his mother and father made him tell the story of everything that had happened all over again, and this time Gay butted in after practically every word, just like old times. But he didn't mind. In fact, he let her tell a lot of it. Why not? After all, most of it was her fault, so she deserved a chance to tell some of it.

When they reached the part about sneaking into Mrs. Pembroke's, his father got to laughing so hard he had to stop the car.

"I shouldn't laugh, but I can just imagine the look on poor Xerxes' face!" he said, wiping his eyes.

Kerby shook his head as he thought of his own narrow escape.

"Well, all I can say is, it's a lucky thing somebody rang Mrs. Pembroke's doorbell when they did, or I'd be in jail now!"

"*I* rang the bell," said Gay.

"*What?*"

"Well, gee whiz, Kerby, who did you *think* rang it?"

He was astounded.

"My gosh, I never even thought about it!"

"I was peeking around the house watching for the postman; and when I saw Mrs. Pembroke come along right after he came, I waited till he left — and then I ran around and rang her bell."

"Why?"

Gay's small face twisted in a puzzled way.

"I don't know. It just seemed like a good idea."

Kerby's father reached back and tweaked her nose.

"Gay, you're a born adventuress. I think you know instinctively the right thing to do in a pinch."

It was wonderful not to have anything to worry about for a change. Kerby enjoyed the unfamiliar feeling all the way home and after they reached home — until his father went outside and brought in the evening paper.

"Look! They've printed Kerby's letter on the front page!"

When Mr. Maxwell said that, Kerby was glancing out the

window toward Bumps's house, wondering if Bumps would make friends again now and let Kerby come back into the club. And as he gazed at Bumps's house, the paper boy threw the evening paper up on Bumps's porch.

At once a horrible realization hit Kerby. Suddenly he could remember with terrible clarity everything he had said in his letter. It was all about Bumps! It called him a Bad Citizen! And Bumps would know, the minute he read it!

"Omigosh!" moaned Kerby. He stared across at Bumps's house, and at the rolled-up newspaper lying on the porch, and for an instant he was tempted. If he could only sneak over, before anyone came out to get it . . . But he shook his head.

"No!" he decided. "I can't go through *that* again!"

But what was he going to do now? When Bumps read that letter — ouch!

11

AT BREAKFAST Mr. Maxwell repeated the advice he had given Kerby about ten times the night before.

"Now, son, you can't avoid Bumps forever — in fact, you can't even avoid him *today,* not when you're bound to meet him at the swimming pool. But I'm sure that if you'll simply march straight up to him and say, 'Bumps, I'm sorry, I wrote that letter when we were both mad, and I hope there's no hard feelings,' you'll find he'll be willing to shake hands and forget about it."

"That's easy for you to say, Dad. It's not your nose!"

"Never mind whose nose it is. If you just march straight up to him and say you're sorry, Bumps is not going to be small about this thing."

By the time Kerby left to walk over to the pool he had decided to take his father's advice — mainly because he could not think of anything better. As his father had said, there was no point in running away. That would not do any good. He could not keep on running away forever. The only thing to do was to walk straight up to Bumps and say . . .

"Bumps, I'm sorry, I wrote that letter when we were both mad, and I hope there's no hard feelings," he muttered, practicing his speech to himself as he left the house by the back door. *"Bumps, I'm sorry, I wrote that letter when we were both mad, and . . ."*

Taking some more of his father's advice, he went through the fence and cut straight across the vacant lot, where Bumps could see him. Of course, maybe with luck Bumps would already be gone, but —

"Hey! Kerby!"

Kerby's heart felt as though somebody had started dribbling it down a basketball court. That was Bumps yelling out of his upstairs window! He did not sound very forgiving, either. He sounded good and mad! Kerby was too frightened to reply — and anyway, Bumps's head disappeared almost immediately. Kerby kept on walking, with prickles running up and down his spine, and practiced one last time.

"Bumps, I'm sorry, I wrote that letter when —"

Bumps came rushing out the side door in his heavy-footed way.

"Hey! I wanna see you!"

"When we were both mad, and I h-hope — Nuts!" cried Kerby, and lit out as fast as he could run.

"Hey! Come back here!"

For once Bumps ran a whole block without stumbling. He began to gain on Kerby. Soon he was right on his heels. He reached out a big hand and grabbed Kerby by the arm. Kerby flew around in an arc, as though they were playing crack-the-whip, and landed in a heap. Bumps stood over him, his cruel nose-twisting fingers twitching.

"You got one coming, and you know it!" he declared.

Kerby lay panting and helpless. But somehow, now that there was no escape, he found the spirit not to whine. Instead, he glared up at Bumps. The heck with it! Let him twist away and get it over with!

"Go ahead, you big bully!" he cried. "If you can't take a little joke —"

"Who says I can't take a little joke?"

"*I* say you can't take a little joke!"

"Well, I can *too* take a little joke if I want to!"

"Well, you don't *look* much like anybody that can take a little joke!"

"Is that so? Well, your letter didn't sound like no little joke anyhow, and I don't think you meant it that way, either!"

98

Bumps had him there. Kerby's silence was an admission.

"Then why did you say I can't take a little joke?" demanded Bumps.

"Well . . . Aw, I don't know!"

Bumps frowned down at him some more.

"All I can say is, you're just lucky you're not gonna get what's coming to you!"

Kerby gaped up at him.

"What do you mean I'm not gonna get what's coming to me?"

" 'Cause you're just not, that's all. My Pop read your letter and said you were right, and so did Ma; so I guess I got to lump it," said Bumps stolidly. "In fact, we're even gonna have a free election for president in the club, now. Me and Fenton were talking about it the other day — before you even wrote your letter, too, so what do you think of *that,* Mr. Smart Guy? Now I want to know something. If I let you come back in the club, who you gonna vote for?"

"Oh, I'll vote for *you,* Bumps!" Kerby assured him in a rush of gratitude.

"Okay. Fenton said if we had one he'd vote for me too, so I'll still be president," said Bumps. "Only now I'll be an *elected* president!"

. . . So the nice box of writing paper you sent me for my birthday has certainly got a lot of use already and I am very glad to have it. Thank you very much.

Love,
KERBY

Kerby sat back with a sigh and looked down at the last of his thank-you letters, the one to Great-aunt Cora. He read it over, and then had the good sense to add a postscript:

P.S. I still have plenty of it left, though.

After all, if he didn't say that, she might send him more next Christmas — and enough was enough.

With his letters out of the way he felt so good that he wanted to go out and take a ride on his new bicycle. He went quietly out into the hall and slipped down the stairs. Gay was in her room reading, and he didn't want to disturb her.

He slipped out the back door, took his bike out of the garage, and rolled it around the side of the house.

When he came around in front, Gay was sitting on the front steps. She looked like somebody waiting for a bus. She didn't say a thing. She just sat there watching him, and hoping. Hope was sticking out all over her.

Kerby glowered at her for a moment. Then he sighed heavily.

"Oh, all right! Get on!"

And off he rode, with his Cousin Gay squealing happily on the handle bars.

About the Author

SCOTT CORBETT is the author of many other Trick books about Kerby and Fenton, including *The Disappearing Dog Trick*, *The Hairy Horror Trick*, and *The Hangman's Ghost Trick*, all available as Apple paperbacks. Mr. Corbett lives in Providence, Rhode Island.

Bring home
SLEEPOVER FRIENDS!

Here's an exciting excerpt from *PATTI'S LUCK #1*, coming in August:

Patti arranged her hair into a row of purple spikes, sort of like the Statue of Liberty's crown. Stephanie's purple curls stuck straight out, as though she'd had an electric shock.

Kate was reading the label on the jar of styling gel. "This stuff stains cloth," she said. "We'd better wash it out before it gets on anything."

Patti went into the bathroom. But she was out in a second.

"No hot water? Let it run for a minute or two," Stephanie told her.

Patti shook her purple head. "No," she said. "There's *no water at all*."

The water main hadn't been repaired when we started home the next morning. Our purple hair was standing straight up.

Donald Foster was in his front yard, fiddling with a lawn mower. "Looking good, girls! Where are your broomsticks?"

Broomsticks, bad luck, witches.... After all that happened at the sleepover, I couldn't help thinking of...the *Beekman curse*. What if Kate's words were right, and the time was right, and the moon and the stars were in the right places?

Truth or dare, scary movies, all-night boy talk—they're all part of SLEEPOVER FRIENDS.

Watch for back-of-the-book information on how *you* can get the official SLEEPOVER FRIENDS Sleepover Kit—everything you need to know to have a great sleepover party!

Coming in August... PATTI'S LUCK Sleepover Friends #1
by Susan Saunders $2.50/$3.50 Can.

◣ Scholastic Books

SLE87